Mr. Messy's guide to
STU... FE

Inspired by life with the
Mr. Men and Little Misses

Illustrated by Adam Hargreaves

No matter what time your first lecture is, you'll always sleep through it.

Little Miss Late

Mr. Greedy's grant cheque stretches until lunchtime.

Mr. Greedy

Mr. Mean

The free plastic badge Mr. Mean
receives helps sway him
in choosing which bank
account to open.

Parents have their uses.
Well, their washing machines do.

Mr. Messy

You know you're a student if:
You've ever written a
cheque for 63p.

BIG BANK

Date _____

Sixty Three
pence

£ 00. 63 p

Mr. Small

Mr. Small.

0026728 927266 2728209

Mr. Small

Never, ever look in
a student's fridge.

Mr. Brave

Mr. Silly thinks paying £75 for a book, sticking it on a shelf, never reading it, and selling it a year later for a tenner is good value for money.

Mr. Clever

Mr. Silly

Mr. Nosey

Only wash dishes when they begin
to develop their own eco-system.

Mr. Lazy chooses his
subject carefully.

Mr. Quiet's enthusiasm for his first term at college instantly evaporates on the arrival of his room-mate.

**You know you're
a student when:**
Pizza is a nutritious meal.

Mr. Skinny

Mr. Mischief

At midnight, fire-extinguishers turn into toys.

To copy from one book = plagiarism.

To copy from many = research.

**Little Miss
Naughty**

**Little Miss
Brainy**

Mr. Clumsy packs for college.

Mr. Clumsy

Mr. Lazy discovers the library is a nice, warm, quiet place to study.

Mr. Lazy

Mr. Rush

It's 4am and your dissertation is due for 9am . . . no problem!

BANK Book

Mr. Greedy

**You know you are
a student when:**
Your rubbish bin is overflowing
but your bank account isn't.

So you borrowed money to go to college, so that you can get a job, so that you can pay back the money you borrowed?

Little Miss Dotty

Mr. Slow

Mr. Slow lives by the motto:

The sooner you fall behind, the more time you'll have to catch up.

Little Miss Scatterbrain uses her initiative when it comes to finding a clean mug.

Little Miss Scatterbrain

Mr. Grumpy

The lecturer says:
'Let's split up into quiet
discussion groups.'

The lecturer means:
'I have a headache!'

Mr. Silly

Mr. Silly can't help finding
traffic cones amusing.

You know you're a student if:
You're in debt by £20,000
before your 20th birthday.

Mr. Worry

Students with cars make
friends easily.

Mr. Uppity

Little Miss Naughty

What not to bring to exams:

1. Pillow
2. Super Soaker
3. Your mother

What not to do in exams:

1. Start a wave
2. Eat the exam paper
3. Heckle

Little Miss Trouble

Exams? What exams?

Mr. Forgetful

Mr. Happy

**You know you're not
a student any more when**: You find a fiver in your pocket you
didn't know you had.